THE BANANA CABANA

Meet

HOWIE

the hotel manager.
Howie likes: trampolines,
running fast, ear wax.
Howie dislikes: silence,
quitters, bubble baths.

Meet

OCTO

at the hotel's front desk.
Octo likes: firm mattresses,
clean teeth, pop-up books.
Octo dislikes: slippery floors,
most condiments, clowns.

First published in Great Britain in 2013 by Hodder Children's Books

Written by Sarah Courtauld
Interior layout by ninataradesign.com

A Catalogue record for this book is available from the British Library.

ISBN: 978 1 444 91390 3

Printed in Spain

The paper and board used in this paperback by Hodder Children's Books are natural
recyclable products made from wood grown in sustainable forests. The manufacturing
processes conform to the environmental regulations of the country of origin.

Hodder Children's Books
A division of Hachette Children's Books
338 Euston Road, London NW1 3BH
An Hachette UK company
www.hachette.co.uk

WHAT COULD POSSIBLY GO WRONG?

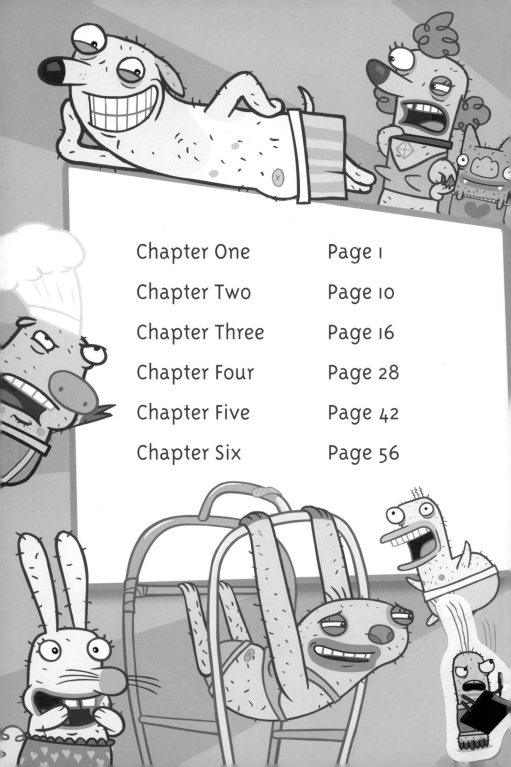

Peace and quiet.
 Ahhh.
 Peace. And. Quiet.
 Octo was all alone in the lobby
of the Banana Cabana.

CHAPTER 1

WELCOME TO THE BANANA CABANA

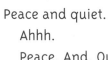

OKIE DONKEY!

 For the last ten minutes,
nothing had exploded. No squirrels had crashed through
the ceiling. No monster trucks had knocked through any of
the walls.
 It was perfect. Just one blue octopus, sitting in the lobby,
thinking about pillows.
 Mmmn, pillows, Octo thought. *I wonder how long this
will—*

YEE — HAAAAAAAAA!

Octo looked up to see Howie at the top of the stairs, sitting on something that looked like a washing machine, probably because it was a washing machine.

'Watch this!' Howie shouted, as he and the washing machine crashed down the stairs, step by step.

BANG! CRASH! WALLOP! SHKRRR!

The machine and Howie crashed at the bottom of the stairs, only narrowly avoiding Shrimp, wearing a pair of sparkly reflective shorts. And only totally destroying the staircase.

'TADA!' said Howie,
bounding over to Octo.

'Er, hi Howie,' Octo gulped.

'Octo!' beamed Howie. 'Whoahhh ... Did you just feel that too?'

'Feel the stairs collapse?' asked Octo.

'No, that urge!' Howie replied. 'That urge ... to do dog stuff!'

'Nope,' said Octo. 'Of course, I don't feel the urge to do octopus stuff either. Unless the urge to do octopus stuff means wanting to remove all possible causes of danger from any given situation.'

'Maybe,' yipped Howie, whose brain was, by now, starting to spin.

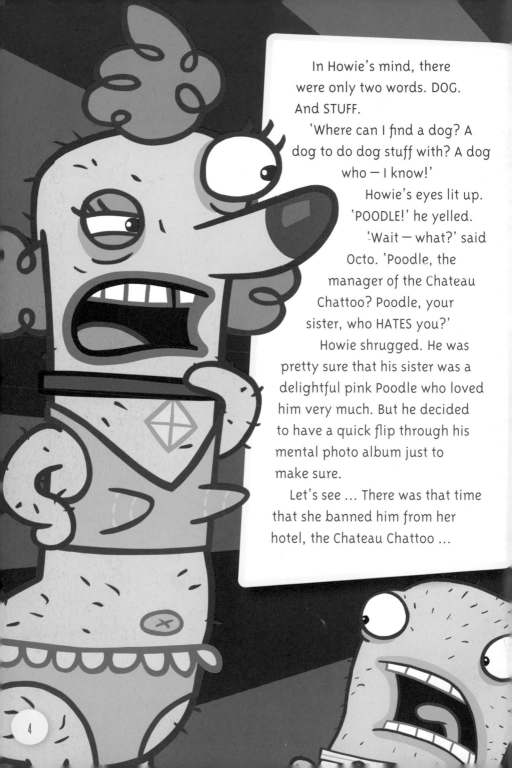

In Howie's mind, there were only two words. DOG. And STUFF.

'Where can I find a dog? A dog to do dog stuff with? A dog who — I know!'

Howie's eyes lit up. 'POODLE!' he yelled.

'Wait — what?' said Octo. 'Poodle, the manager of the Chateau Chattoo? Poodle, your sister, who HATES you?'

Howie shrugged. He was pretty sure that his sister was a delightful pink Poodle who loved him very much. But he decided to have a quick flip through his mental photo album just to make sure.

Let's see … There was that time that she banned him from her hotel, the Chateau Chattoo …

... The time she stole all the food from the Banana Cabana with a giant claw, hoping that he and his friends would abandon it, so she could take over ...

… The time that she attacked the Banana Cabana with a pirate ship …

'Yep!' Howie said to Octo. 'Poodle is great and I'm going to do dog stuff with her!'

So Howie raced off in search of his beloved sister Poodle, yelling:

DOG STUFF! DOG STUFF! DOG STUFF! TREE! OW! DOG STUFF! DOG STUFF!

Octo looked at the washing machine in the middle of the hall. And the small, but not insignificant pile of animals who had tripped over the washing machine, and were now forming a highly dangerous-looking guest pile.

There were dangers everywhere at the Banana Cabana.

And Octo wasn't even thinking about Radiation Rooster.

Hey, thanks a lot! Microwave oven, anyone?

The more Octo thought about it, the more danger he could see *all around him*.

There was the kitchen, which was full of knives ...

... the pool, which was full of water ...

... the air, which was full of — who even knew what the air was full of?

And that was just inside. What about outside? Outside was the sky! Who knew what could happen when the sky was involved?

Danger! thought Octo, jiggling with fear.

CHAPTER 2

Over at the Chateau Chattoo, Howie crashed through the door. He was saving all his energy for dog stuff — that's why he'd only chased his own tail 322 times on the way over.

'Hey, sis!' said Howie. As always, Poodle was delighted to see her brother. He could tell by the way her eyes narrowed, and she stepped backwards, and pointed to the signs she'd put up everywhere. Signs that read:

NO HOWIE

NO BROTHERS OF POODLE ALLOWED

NO ONE WELCOME WHOSE NAME SOUNDS LIKE 'OWIE'

HOWIE, LEAVE ALREADY

HOWIE, DO YOU REALLY NOT GET IT YET?

NO, HOWIE, SERIOUSLY, YOU'RE NOT ALLOWED

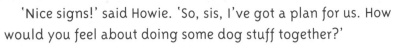

'Nice signs!' said Howie. 'So, sis, I've got a plan for us. How would you feel about doing some dog stuff together?'

'Dog stuff?' shrieked Poodle.

'Yeah, dog stuff!' said Howie. 'You know, chasing our own tails, and running around in circles, and accidentally setting fire to ourselves and—'

'STOP!' shouted Poodle. 'I do not want to do dog stuff with you,' she said, wondering for the 1,543,187th time how she and Howie were actually related.

Poodle referred to her mental list:

What Howie And I Have in Common
We Are, Unfortunately, Related.

What We Don't Have In Common
EVERYTHING ELSE
'I'd rather sandpaper my own eyeballs than do dog stuff with you,' she said.

Trust me, it is less fun than it sounds.

Poodle was hoping to make her point clear. Crystal clear.

'So,' said Howie, 'is that a yes?'

'No!' screamed Poodle.

'Pleeeasssseee?' asked Howie.

'Never!' Poodle yelled. She had evil plans to take over the Banana Cabana to work on.

'Are you SURE?' asked Howie sadly.

'For the last time, I don't want to hang out with my goofball brother!' said Poodle.

'Wait. What?' said Howie, his eyes lighting up like the time he accidentally swallowed a box of lightbulbs.

I have a *brother*? And he's a *GOOFBALL*?!

'I'm bored of this conversation,' sighed Poodle, walking away.

'I just don't get sisters,' said Howie. 'I wish I did have a brother, to play games with, and tell jokes to, and give half my hotel to ...'

Poodle stopped in her tracks.

'Give half his hotel to?' she muttered. 'Heee heee heee hee hee,' she giggled. A cunning plan was forming in her mind.

'HEE HEEE HAAA HAAA!' cackled Batty, her sidekick.

'HEEEEE HEEE ... Wait! I don't get it.'

BATTY
hench-animal

Poodle looked down at her small, not-so-smart hench-animal, and sighed.

Hmmmn. I need someone's help with this plan, she thought. Batty was good for some things, like being fired out of cannons, or watching ballet. But for this she needed someone quite different ...

'Got it!' she giggled again. She had a quite brilliant plan.

'Heee hee hee!' Batty cackled. 'Wait. I *still* don't get it.'

CHAPTER 3

Back at the Banana Cabana, How̶ to his friends

Meet

BUNNY

the Hotel Activities Director.
Bunny likes: princesses,
stickers, rainbows.
She dislikes: slow days,
broken mirrors, armpits.

'So,' said Bunny, 'at the Chateau Chattoo, Poodle has actual "No Howie Allowed" signs?'

'Yep!' said Howie. 'She's always thinking of me!'

'Uhh, Howie,' Bunny replied — but before she could say anything else, she was interrupted by a polite cough.

'Harumph,' said a stranger, tapping Howie on the shoulder. 'I'm looking for my long-lost brother. About as tall as you. He looks like this ...'

He held up a mirror to Howie's face.

'Oh, and he answers to the name ...'

'Please say Howie, please say Howie, please say Howie, please say Howie pleasesayHowiepleasesayHowiepleasesay HowiepleasesayHowiepleasesayHowiepleasesay HowiepleasesayHowiepleasesayHowiepleasesay HowiepleasesayHowiepleasesayHowiepleasesayHowie ...' said Howie.

'OK,' said the stranger. 'Howie.'

'Wait,' said Howie. 'That's ...

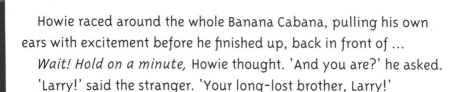

Howie raced around the whole Banana Cabana, pulling his own ears with excitement before he finished up, back in front of ...

Wait! Hold on a minute, Howie thought. 'And you are?' he asked.

'Larry!' said the stranger. 'Your long-lost brother, Larry!'

'LARRY!' said Howie, sweeping Larry right off the ground. He gave him a huge hug. 'I didn't know I'd lost you! Or that you even existed! Wow — you must have been really lost!'

'Er, Howie?' said Larry. 'Could you put me down? I got this little fear of heights ...'

Howie obediently dropped Larry.

Crack!

'... and, er broken bones,' said Larry, wincing, from the floor.

'Right,' said Howie. 'We used to tease you about that! I'm sure we did. Didn't we?'

'Ummmmmmm ...' said Larry.

Howie turned to Bunny and Octo, beaming. 'Guys!' he said. 'It's my long-lost younger brother, Harry!'

'*Older* brother. And it's Larry. But the important thing is, we're brothers again. Right? Brothers, who share stuff? Right, brother?'

'Yeah, Barry!' said Howie, giving him a huge, brotherly hug.

'It's LARRY!' said Larry.

'Larry. Sure. Let's share stuff — like this list!'

Howie pulled a little square of paper from his pocket, and unfolded it. 'When I was younger,' he said excitedly, 'I made a list of stuff I would do with my brother, if I had one. Number one: make each other laugh till juice shoots out our noses!'

'Well, then, let's go, little brother!' said Larry, and they raced off on a high-speed search for juice.

As Bunny watched them go, she frowned. 'Is it just me, or does something seem wrong here?'

'Oh, it's wrong all right,' Octo replied. 'On a list of stuff to do, shooting juice out of your nose is number six, five tops!'

'Hmmmmn,' said Bunny. There was a mystery here, and she was going to get to the bottom of it.

Meanwhile, Howie and Larry were telling each other stories, but it was weird. Howie was telling his very best stories, which always made Octo giggle helplessly. But instead of the sound of helpless giggling, all he could hear was Larry, sucking on a straw.

'And then,' Howie said, 'he says, how about a jelly sandwich?!!!'

'Huh,' said Larry.

'Still no nostril juice?' said Howie. Then he had a brainwave. A tickly kind of brainwave.

At that exact moment, the chef of the Banana Cabana came striding through the lounge, carrying a cake.

Piggy's cake had three layers, each more delicious
than the last. As Piggy strutted past, with his head
held high ... Howie dived on to Larry.

'TICKLE FIGHT!!!!' he yelled.

They tumbled to the floor, Larry sprayed
a jet of juice through his nose, and ...

YAAAOUUUWWW!

'SUCCESS!' Howie
shouted happily. 'The
juice shot out your
nostrils! OK, what's next
on the list?'

'Er, taking me to the
hospital?' said Larry.

'Number Two ...
Making up hilarious
nicknames. Let's go!'

Making up nicknames was hilarious, and Howie and Larry thought they were pretty good at it. There was Beaky McBeak

Snouty McSnout

and Slowy McSlowSlow.

'Hey,' said Larry, nudging
Howie, as Bunny walked into the lobby.
'Here comes Toothy McTooth. Hey, looking good, Toothy McTooth!'
'Toothy McTooth, huh?' said Bunny. She was not impressed.

Bunny didn't have a nickname for Larry. What she did have for him
was a swift kick to the pants. 'YEOUW!' Larry yelled.

'OK! Next item,' said Howie. 'Burying ourselves in sand!'
'Great,' Larry muttered to himself. 'As if being your brother wasn't
painful enough already.' So he buried Howie in sand, and even
poured a bit of extra sand on his head with a spade.

'My turn!' said Howie. Howie was going to do this one in style.

Larry nervously gnawed on his toenails as Howie ran off into the
distance and then returned with a ...

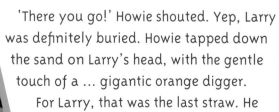

'There you go!' Howie shouted. Yep, Larry
was definitely buried. Howie tapped down
the sand on Larry's head, with the gentle
touch of a ... gigantic orange digger.

For Larry, that was the last straw. He
marched straight over to the Chateau
Chattoo.

THAT'S IT!

he yelled to Poodle, bursting in through the door. 'I quit! I'm not being Howie's fake brother ANY MORE!'

'What?' Poodle hissed, turning on him. 'You can't quit. We have a deal! I get to take over the hotel, and you get to be centre stage there every night.'

'But he's driving me crazy!' said Larry. 'I give up.'

'Cut it out!' Poodle replied. 'It's only a matter of time before he gives you half of the Banana Cabana.'

'But how do you know your scheme will even work?' Larry asked Poodle.

'Because Howie is very sharing!' said Poodle. 'There's nothing more he'd love to do than share his hotel with a brother.'

'And,' said Batty, 'because pretending is what you do best.'

'You're right. Because I am an actor!' said Larry, in a very actory way. 'And so I will act!'

He stood in the doorway, and cleared his throat.

'To be or not to be, that is the quest—'

BANG!

Poodle slammed the front door of the Chateau Chattoo, and 'Larry' went on his way.

CHAPTER 4

Che-lo-wa, che-lo-wa, che-lo-wa chely
Don't shave a banana with your eyes!

Later that night, Larry was in the lounge, watching Narwhal singing away on the stage.

Narwhal ... According to Narwhal:
He's the best crooner in town, baby.

'Huh,' Larry muttered to himself, 'I'm ten times more talented than Horny McHornHorn over there. Just got to keep being nice ...'

'Larry!' said Howie, tumbling into the lounge at high speed. 'Food fight? Come on! What do you say?'

'Sounds ... fun,' said Larry, as if the word 'fun' meant 'very painful indeed' or 'just like going to the dentist'.

'OK!' said Howie, splatting Larry with food from a sauce-laden spoon.

SPLAT! SPLAT! SPLAT!

After three splats, Larry was covered in sauce. He steeled himself. *Must be nice to Howie,* he thought.

'Bedtime!' said the actor, later that night. 'Now I can go to sleep,' he muttered. 'Finally some time alone.'

'Alone?' said Howie, springing up from behind him. 'I couldn't do that to my brother! You're bunking with me!'

'But Howie, *I'm* your room-mate,' said Octo, shuffling over to them, and looking even bluer than usual. 'Where am *I* going to sleep?'

'It's all right, I've figured it out!' said Howie. 'We can all fit!'

Up in Howie's bedroom, Howie showed the others where they were sleeping. There were three bunks, all on top of each other.

'You're family, Larry, so you get the top bunk,' Howie explained.

'Er, remember, I've got that fear of heights,' Larry said with a gulp.

'That's OK! Once the light's out, you can't tell how high you are!' said Howie.

Howie gave his long-lost brother a little swing and chucked him up into his bunk, then switched out the light. It was dark. And Larry was high up. His teeth chattered. His heart beat like a crazy drum.

Too high, too high, too high! he thought to himself. But he knew he had to play along. *I have to make this fun for Howie.*

He wasn't the only one on the bunk bed who was unhappy. Octo was feeling left out. Was he still Howie's best friend? It wasn't just that Howie had started calling him Army McArmArm. He and Howie always whispered fun stories to each other in the night, just like Howie and Larry were doing.

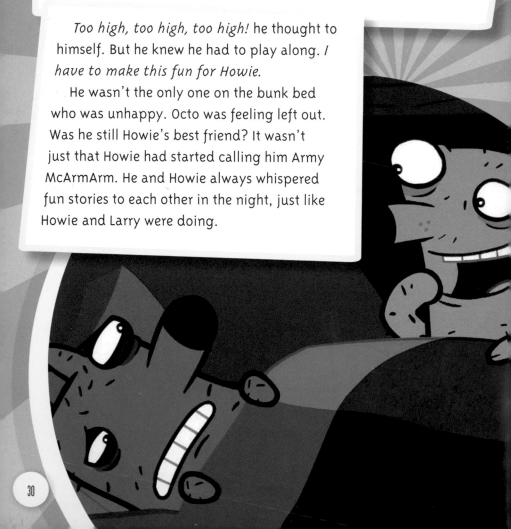

It was good that Howie had found his brother, Octo thought, but he felt a little bit like he was losing his friend.

Oh well, thought Octo. *Howie's doing brother stuff. Maybe I should try to do some Octo stuff. Like ... making everything safe. Safe and Sound.*

He made his own list:

Octo Stuff
1) Make everything safe.
2) Keep going.
3) Is it safe enough?
4) You can never be too safe!

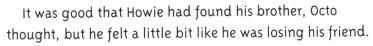

Then he fell fast asleep, and dreamed beautiful dreams about Super Safe Safety Tape.

The next morning, Larry woke up yawning. He was so sleeeeepy. Howie had stayed up nearly all night, telling him story after story after story after story after story after story …

'Urghh,' he yawned, shuffling into the lounge for breakfast, and sleepily looked at the …

'Free food!' he cried, instantly awake. 'An actor's dream! Nachos! Spaghetti! Melons! Tiny dips! Soup! Chips! Cheese straws!'

On the other side of the dining room, Bunny was watching him.

'Don't you think it's weird that Howie's never mentioned his long-lost brother before?' she asked Sloth.

Meet

SLOTH

the slowest bellhop you'll ever meet.
Sloth likes: lounging,
Howie, makeovers.
Sloth dislikes: long walks, line
dancing, old cheese.

'I know,' said Sloth. 'It is weird! And have you noticed that Larry doesn't look like Howie, or sound like Howie, or act like Howie?'

They looked over at him suspiciously.

'Come to Papa!' Larry said, as he swallowed a five-foot-high cake in one gulp.

'At least, he doesn't act like him *most* of the time,' Sloth said.

'Well, I think there's something strange going on,' said Bunny.

I guess there's no one quite like Howie, Sloth thought to herself, drifting into a lovely Howie daydream.

CWWWWWWWWWWWWWWWWWWW

'… Whoah! Octo? What are you DOING?'

Sloth snapped out of her daydream to find Octo doing something weird to her cart. Very weird indeed. He appeared to be decorating it with deflated balloons.

'Octo, what is this?' asked Sloth.

'Safety first!' said Octo.

'Are these airbags?' said Sloth. 'Wait. This is ridic—'

POiNNNG!

'Octo!' came Sloth's muffled voice. 'OCTO!!!!'

Octo ticked an item off his list, and went on his way, pleased with a job well done.

A moment later, Bunny caught up with Howie in the lobby.

'Howie, are you sure Larry is who he says he is?' she asked. 'You don't even look alike!'

'Not true,' said Howie with a smile. 'We have identical birthmarks, under our underarms!'

'Er, Howie,' said Bunny. 'That's … raspberry jam.'

'Oh,' said Howie, licking it away. 'Delicious!'

'I mean, there's so much you don't know about him!' said Bunny.

'Larry is SO my brother,' Howie replied. 'That's why he's going to join me in the bestest most amazing two-dog stunt EVER!'

'Really? Larry agreed to that?' asked Bunny.

'Yes! Probably … for sure! As soon as I tell him!' And Howie sped off to find Larry.

In the lounge, Larry was treading the boards.

'Soon, all this will be mine. Mine!' he declared. 'The boards! The backdrops! The fake palm trees! The slightly stained curtains!'

He couldn't contain his excitement. Howie *must* be just about to hand over his half of the hotel. He could feel it in his bones.

'Guess what we're going to do next, bro?' said Howie, who had sped into the dining room at top speed.

'Share the hotel?' asked Larry.

'Yep! Right after we perform the bestest most amazing two-dog stunt ever!'

'A stunt?'

'Yeah, a really dangerous one too!' said Howie.

'Sure, maybe one day,' said Larry, edging away from Howie.

'I think we can do better than "one day",' said Howie, grinning. 'It's happening TO-DAY!'

'Today?' said Larry. He gulped.
'Come on outside!' yelled Howie,
grabbing Larry's arm. 'Just to check,
you have used crutches before, right?'

Out in the sunshine, the stunt vehicle looked surprisingly reassuring.

'Phew,' said Larry. 'So we're on a bicycle. We're on the ground at least.'

'Sure,' said Howie excitedly. 'Until the loop-de-loop!'

'The what-de-what?'

'The loop-de-loop!'

'So we go upside down?!'

'Until we're airborne,' said Howie.

'AIRBORNE?!' shrieked Larry.

'That's when the helicopter blades kick in.'

'HELICOPTER BLADES?!'

Larry was jittering. He was sweating. He was trying hard not to faint.

'You can do this,' he whispered to himself. 'You're going to headline at the hotel. A new career! Free meals. Visualise, Larry, visualise.'

'And then we just have to ignite the rockets,' explained Howie.

'Rockets? ROCKETS?!?!' Larry yelled.

'If you know a better way to defy gravity, I'd sure like to see it,' said Howie.

As Larry ran off to throw up in the bushes, Howie looked on, pleased as punch.

'He seems really excited about the stunt,' Howie said to himself.

Meanwhile, Octo was making the kitchen completely safe. He had confiscated all of Piggy's knives, and he was feeling pretty pleased with the move. He hadn't *quite* convinced Piggy though.

'No sharpy sharp things!' Piggy shouted, jumping up and down, purple with rage.

'That's right,' said Octo. 'Knives are dangerous. You could hurt yourself.'

'So, many-armed smarty pants,' said Piggy, 'how Piggy supposed to chop carrots for Piggy-perfect carrot cake? With scoopy thing?' And he banged the carrots with his wooden spoon, to make his point. 'Many-armed wiggly thing!' Piggy roared.

'Meet Louis,' replied Octo calmly. 'He's a woodchuck.'

Piggy looked on as Octo pulled open a cupboard to reveal a woodchuck, complete with two huge, jutting front teeth.

'Hey,' said Louis.

'He'll safely chew up everything you need,' said Octo.

Louis shrugged. 'It's a gift,' he said.

With the knives dealt with, Octo went off to take care of the BIG ONE. He'd been thinking a lot about this. It could happen any day. The sky could simply fall! So Octo had come up with a practical solution. He was going to cover the hotel in pillows.

As he sat on the roof, gluing on pillow after pillow, he could just hear Howie, over the other side of the Banana Cabana, making a grand announcement ...

CHAPTER 5

'Welcome!' said Howie, beaming from the top of the stunt track. He looked down at the crowd below.

'Our gravity-defying, two-dog brother stunt will soon begin!' he announced.

Howie was practically glowing with excitement. He and Larry were *The Danger Brothers*! What could possibly go wrong?

Unfortunately, The Actor Pretending To Be Larry was thinking exactly the same question. *What could possibly go wrong?*

'Let's see ... there's the loop-de-loop ... and then there's the rockets.'

He looked at the stunt track, and gulped. His mouth was dry. Spotting Poodle in the audience, Larry ran up to her.

'That's it! I'm done!' he said. 'Being Nutty McNutbar's brother is just too dangerous!'

Poodle leaped up from her seat and took his arm.

'Come with me, brother,' she said menacingly, and dragged him over to some bushes.

'Listen, brother,' she hissed, 'just do the stunt, get the hotel, then you can take over Narwhal's stage. Get it?'

Larry nodded glumly. His teeth were still chattering uncontrollably.

'Now break a leg!' Poodle said. She gave him a forceful push in the direction of the stunt. He walked over to it, gulped, and, turning a pale shade of greeny-grey, began to climb up the tall wooden tower to the start position ...

wasn't the only one who had heard Poodle's little pep talk.

'I knew it!' said Bunny. 'I knew hiding in the bushes was a great idea! And I knew Poodle would be behind this! Ha!'

She and Sloth shook off their leaves-of-disguise and leaped out of the bushes.

'We've got to stop the stunt!' said Sloth. 'They're already putting on their helmets!'

'I'm all over it,' said Bunny, pulling a couple of saws out of her polka dot pants.

'Wow, that girl is ready for anything,' said Sloth.

At the very top of the track, Larry shivered like he'd never shivered before.

'Hello!' yelled Howie to the audience below. 'We are the Danger Brothers! And you are about to see the bestest, most dangerous stunt ever performed.'

The crowd cheered.

'And once this amazing feat of derring-do is accomplished, I will have done everything on my Stuff To Do With My Brother list. And so … I've made a new list, called More Things To Do With My Brother!'

Larry looked at it, horrified. He caught sight of the words 'danger', 'clouds', 'mountain top' and 'canine land speed record.'

He was starting to feel very, very dizzy.

'And,' Howie proudly went on, 'because my brother is way more important to me than some silly hotel, I'm shutting down the Banana Cabana—'

'WHAT?' shouted Larry. 'Now I really QUIT!' He yanked off his Dirk Danger helmet, and tossed it away.

'But we're the Danger Brothers!' gasped Howie.

'I'm not your brother!' yelled the actor.

'Sure you are, we have nicknames, and matching stunt uniforms ...'

'I'm an actor,' said Larry. 'Your sister hired me.'

'Wait — because ... the real Larry couldn't be here?' asked Howie, confused.

'There IS no real Larry!'

'So what's his name then,' said Howie. 'Barry? Jerry? Gary? Mary?'

'Don't you get it? You have NO BROTHER! All you have is an evil sister who wants your hotel.'

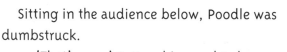

Sitting in the audience below, Poodle was dumbstruck.

'That's you,' Batty whispered to her, proudly, giving her a nudge.

'So long, Howie,' said The Actor Who Would Never More Be Known As Larry. And then, in a final, brilliant, theatrical gesture, he jumped from the stunt track.

That turned out to be a mistake. It was, he had forgotten, quite a long way down.

OWWWWWWWWWWWWWWWW

As Larry limped away, Howie was looking forlorn.

'I have no brother,' he said to himself. 'And no most amazingly dangerous two-dog stunt.'

'Hold on, Howie!' came a shout, and one blue tentacle, and then another blue tentacle, appeared over the ledge of the stunt track.

'I may not be your brother, but I am your best friend. And even though this looks like the opposite of safe, I want to do this with you!'

Howie grabbed Octo's tentacle with his paw, and grinned.

'Ready, buddy?' he asked.

'You bet!' said Octo.

So Howie pedalled forwards, the bike shot over the edge of the start, and into the most amazingly dangerous, death-defying, sanity-challenging, vertigo-inducing stunt ... ever!

WHOOOOORRRRHHHH!

yelled Octo, who had never had a deeper sense of why he liked working at a desk.

'I've never regretted anything so quickly!' Octo yelled, as they careered down a death-defying slope.

'Welcome to my world, brother!' Howie yelled back, as they gathered speed.

They sped down a vertical
track, and were headed
straight for the loop-
de-loop, just as
Bunny finished
sawing it
in half.

They
careered
around the
loop-de-loop,
and shot through
the hole, and went
rocketing into the air.

'Oops,' said Bunny.

YARHHHHA!!!

They bounced off the hotel's roof pillows ...

'Safety first!' yelled Octo.

... and then off the Banana Cabana's banana ... and through the skies ...

… until they landed in the hotel swimming pool with an almighty splash. They'd made it.

Just barely.

'Hey, you know what I just realised?' Howie said, panting.

'We're … still alive?' answered Octo, trembling.

'Well, yes, but also that ... I don't need a brother! You're like the best brother I could ever have!'

Octo smiled.

'And I can do everything on my new list with you!'

Octo looked down at the list. It was a very, very long list.

CHAPTER 6

That night, everything was back to normal in the Banana Cabana.

Octo sat behind the front desk, telling Howie a funny story, as Piggy strode through the lobby, carrying his most recent extraordinary cake creation.

'Piggy cake genius,' Piggy muttered, holding the beautiful cake in front of him. 'This time, cakey perfection.'

'And then,' Octo said, 'he says, "How about a jelly sandwich?"'

'HAAAAA!' Howie laughed. He spluttered. He tried to swallow his juice, but—

WHOAHHHH!

'Great story,' said Howie. 'OK, my turn—'

'H-hhharumph.'

There was a small polite cough. A small polite cough that belonged to a small purple bat.

'Batty?' said Howie.

'Er, I just thought you should know, er, that Poodle found your long-lost family tree.'

Batty looked down at the ground.

'My long-lost family tree?' said Howie hopefully. He was imagining the best long-lost family tree ever, with Cap'n Fizzy's soda hanging from the branches like magical fizzy fruit.

'And er, it, er, seems I'm your long-lost cousin!' Batty said.

'Really? I always wanted a long-lost cousin!' said Howie, his eyes lighting up. 'I even have a list! Number one thing to do with my cousin: laugh till juice shoots out our noses. Me first!'

Howie took a big gulp of juice, and laughed, and SPLOOOOSH — Batty was covered in cold, sticky juice from head to wing.

'I have a cousin! This is great! This is just the beginning!' shouted Howie.

Batty was not looking quite so excited. He looked down Howie's list. The words 'gravity' and 'defying' seemed to show up a lot.

Uh oh, thought Batty.

'Welcome to the family!' said Octo.

DVD out now!

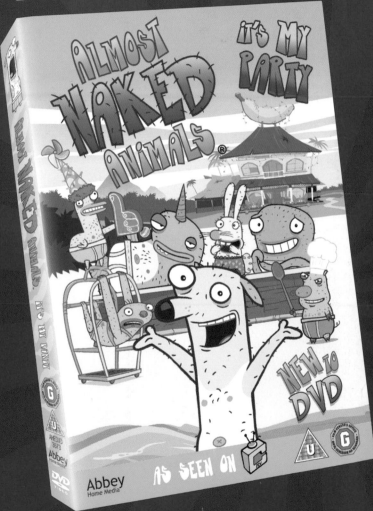